This book belongs to:

_____

_____

Twelve Haunted Rooms of Halloween

Illustrated by
Macky Pamintuan

STERLING CHILDREN'S BOOKS
New York

Through the first haunted doorway
I peeked right in to see . . .

A bat hanging from a bare tree.

Through the second haunted doorway
I peeked right in to see . . .
Two wicked witches,
And a bat hanging from a bare tree.

**Through the third haunted doorway
I peeked right in to see . . .**

Three black cats,
Two wicked witches,
And a bat hanging from a bare tree.

Through the fourth haunted doorway
I peeked right in to see . . .

Four skeletons,
Three black cats,
Two wicked witches,
And a bat hanging from a bare tree.

Through the fifth haunted doorway
I peeked right in to see . . .

Five jack-o-lanterns!
Four skeletons,
Three black cats,
Two wicked witches,
And a bat hanging from a bare tree.

Through the sixth haunted doorway
I peeked right in to see . . .

Six ghosts a-*BOOOO*-ing,
Five jack-o-lanterns!
Four skeletons,
Three black cats,
Two wicked witches,
And a bat hanging from a bare tree.

Through the seventh haunted doorway
I peeked right in to see . . .

Seven goblins growling,
Six ghosts a-**BOOOO**-ing,
Five jack-o-lanterns!
Four skeletons,
Three black cats,
Two wicked witches,
And a bat hanging from a bare tree.

Through the eighth haunted doorway
I peeked right in to see . . .

Eight werewolves howling,
Seven goblins growling,
Six ghosts a-*BOOOO*-ing,
Five jack-o-lanterns!
Four skeletons,
Three black cats,
Two wicked witches,
And a bat hanging from a bare tree.

**Through the ninth haunted doorway
I peeked right in to see . . .**

Nine zombies dancing,
Eight werewolves howling,
Seven goblins growling,
Six ghosts a-*BOOOO*-ing,
Five jack-o-lanterns!
Four skeletons,
Three black cats,
Two wicked witches,
And a bat hanging from a bare tree.

Through the tenth haunted doorway
I peeked right in to see . . .

Ten monsters leaping,
Nine zombies dancing,
Eight werewolves howling,
Seven goblins growling,
Six ghosts a-**BOOOO**-ing,
Five jack-o-lanterns!
Four skeletons,
Three black cats,
Two wicked witches,
And a bat hanging from a bare tree.

**Through the twelfth haunted doorway
I peeked right in to see . . .**

Twelve trick-or-treaters,
Eleven spiders spinning,
Ten monsters leaping,
Nine zombies dancing,
Eight werewolves howling,
Seven goblins growling,
Six ghosts a-*BOOOO*-ing,
Five jack-o-lanterns!
Four skeletons,
Three black cats,
Two wicked witches,
And a bat hanging from a bare tree.

Through the eleventh haunted doorway
I peeked right in to see . . .

Eleven spiders spinning,
Ten monsters leaping,
Nine zombies dancing,
Eight werewolves howling,
Seven goblins growling,
Six ghosts a-*BOOOO*-ing,
Five jack-o-lanterns!
Four skeletons,
Three black cats,
Two wicked witches,
And a bat hanging from a bare tree.

BEW

3 mice

3 spell books

3 voodoo dolls

The silly monsters also hid these items.
Can you find them throughout the haunted house?

3 gargoyles

2 snakes

For Ali
—M.P.

STERLING CHILDREN'S BOOKS
New York

An Imprint of Sterling Publishing
387 Park Avenue South
New York, NY 10016

Library of Congress Cataloging-in-Publication Data Available

Lot#:
2 4 6 8 10 9 7 5 3 1
03/11

Published by Sterling Publishing Co., Inc.
387 Park Avenue South, New York, NY 10016
Text © 2011 by Sterling Publishing Co., Inc. Illustrations © 2011 by Macky Pamintuan
Distributed in Canada by Sterling Publishing
c/o Canadian Manda Group, 165 Dufferin Street
Toronto, Ontario, Canada M6K 3H6
Distributed in the United Kingdom by GMC Distribution Services
Castle Place, 166 High Street, Lewes, East Sussex, England BN7 1XU
Distributed in Australia by Capricorn Link (Australia) Pty. Ltd.
P.O. Box 704, Windsor, NSW 2756, Australia

Printed in China

Sterling ISBN 978-1-4027-7935-0

For information about custom editions, special sales, premium and
corporate purchases, please contact Sterling Special Sales
Department at 800-805-5489 or specialsales@sterlingpublishing.com.